Daniela Drescher

In the Land
of Fairies

Floris Books

In spring the woodland fairies dance
And cast their spell
Turning to green the trees and plants.

By night the Owl, still wakeful, keeps
His eyes alert,
Watching while all the forest sleeps.

The cautious fox hears every sound,
By night and day,
Creeping with care across the ground.

The dusk brings deer into the glade
Where flowers grow,
As dappled light gives way to shade.

Midsummer time, a magic night,
So full of life,
Now fairies dress the woods with light.

The birds now fill each place with song,
    Each bush and tree,
Their voices mingling all day long.

With leaf-fall, every creature stores
Its winter food
While round the woodland autumn roars.

Among the tree-roots, down below,
Nuts, berries, grain
Are safely kept beneath the snow.

As snowflakes fall, the twigs are bowed,
Their heads are low,
But Robin's song still echoes loud.

First published in German under the title
Komm mit ins Elfenland by Verlag Urachhaus
First published in English in 2004 by Floris Books
Third impression 2007

© 2004 Verlag Freies Geistesleben & Urachhaus GmbH, Stuttgart
English version © 2004 Floris Books
15 Harrison Gardens, Edinburgh
www.florisbooks.co.uk

British Library CIP Data available
ISBN 978-086315-450-8
Printed in Poland